The Dream Team

Lee Aucoin, *Creative Director*
Jamey Acosta, *Senior Editor*
Heidi Fiedler, *Editor*
Produced and designed by
Denise Ryan & Associates
Illustration © Alasdair Bright
Rachelle Cracchiolo, *Publisher*

Teacher Created Materials

5301 Oceanus Drive
Huntington Beach, CA 92649-1030
http://www.tcmpub.com
Paperback: ISBN: 978-1-4333-5646-9
Library Binding: ISBN: 978-1-4807-1745-9
© 2014 Teacher Created Materials

Written by
Bill Condon

Illustrated by
Alasdair Bright

Contents

Chapter One

The Team 3

Chapter Two

The Game. 9

Chapter Three

After the Game 15

Chapter Four

Training 21

Chapter Five

Soccer Stars. 27

Chapter One

The Team

Rebecca wanted to find something her friends could do together. One day, she saw an ad on the gym bulletin board.

JUNIOR PLAYERS WANTED FOR SOCCER LEAGUE

Rebecca thought her friends Manny, Silvio, Rosa, Nuong, and Camilla might be interested. *Wouldn't it be cool if we all played soccer together?* she thought.

The next day, Rebecca asked her friends if they wanted to join a soccer team, and they all said yes. Their teacher, Ms. Dunleavy, said she would be their coach.

"The first thing we need to do is choose a team name. Does anyone have any ideas?" asked Ms. Dunleavy.

Six hands shot up.

"Me, me!" the students cried.

Ms. Dunleavy looked at Rebecca. "Since this was your idea, you can choose the name."

"Let's call our team The Caterpillars. I like caterpillars!" Rebecca said.

"That's a great name!" Ms. Dunleavy said. "Caterpillars become something else—something surprising. You'll be every bit as good as the Tigers and the Lions," she told them. "You'll be faster than the Panthers and too smart for the Rhinos. The Caterpillars will be a dream team!"

The first game was only a few days away, and everyone was very excited. Their uniforms were brand new—and green, just like caterpillars. Their cleats were shiny and clean. Nuong and Silvio had even written a song for them. The team sang it as they waited for the game to start:

We're the Caterpillars, yes, we are.
We're the best, and we'll go far!
We kick the ball so straight and true.
We're gonna Caterpillar you!

Chapter Two

The Game

Finally, it was time to play the first game of the season. During the first five minutes, the score was close. The Anacondas had scored one goal. The Caterpillars were looking for their first goal.

The players could see their parents cheering on the sidelines.

"Go! Go, Anacondas!"

"Go! Go, Caterpillars!"

Then, the Anacondas poured on the pressure. They ran fast and hard, scoring goal after goal. The Anaconda fans cheered louder.

Suddenly, Rebecca had the ball at her feet. The goal was wide open. She was going to score!

"Go! Go, Caterpillars! Come on, Rebecca!" cheered the crowd.

"Oh, no!" Rebecca tripped over her laces, and the ball slipped away.

A few minutes later, Manny had the ball. He was running like a champion. Well, almost like a champion. The Anacondas didn't try to stop him, but the Caterpillars' parents did.

"Manny, you're going the wrong way!" they yelled. But he kept running until he scored a goal—for the Anacondas. By half time, the Caterpillars were feeling very unhappy.

"I don't think I like soccer anymore," said Manny.

"We're not very good," Nuong added.

"We're a disaster!" Camilla said.

"Ms. Dunleavy?" Rosa raised her hand.

"Yes, Rosa?"

"Would it be all right if I quit our team and I played for the Anacondas in the second half? I'd rather be on the winning side."

"No, Rosa. That would not be all right."

"'But it's embarrassing," Rosa said.

"Cheer up." Ms. Dunleavy smiled encouragingly. "I'm sure we'll do a lot better in the second half."

Chapter Three

After the Game

They had hoped to do better, but the Caterpillars lost the game badly. Afterward, the players and their families had a picnic lunch. Ms. Dunleavy came, too. No one talked about their terrible score or the mistakes they had made. They tried to remember it was only their first game.

Nuong's dad stood up and raised his glass in the air. "Let's hear it for the Caterpillars! They made it through their first game!" When the cheering stopped, Ms. Dunleavy began to sing the team song. One by one, everyone joined in, and the Caterpillars felt like winners.

A week later, the team played its second game. This time, they were up against the Cougars, one of the best teams in the league.

Ms. Dunleavy gave the Caterpillars some helpful advice: "Manny, keep your eyes open when you kick the ball. That's why you keep missing it. Camilla, try not to duck when the ball comes your way. I promise it won't hurt you. Silvio, don't leave the field if your pants get splashed with mud. Nuong, don't stop playing to comb your hair. The same goes for you, Rosa. And Rebecca, don't turn your back to watch the game being played on the field behind you."

"Even if the other game is more interesting, Ms. Dunleavy?"

"Yes, Rebecca, even then."

Once again, their parents cheered them on. "Go! Go Caterpillars!"

But the players fumbled and stumbled. They tried to kick the ball and missed. They bumped into one another and fell. Meanwhile, the Cougars scored goal after goal.

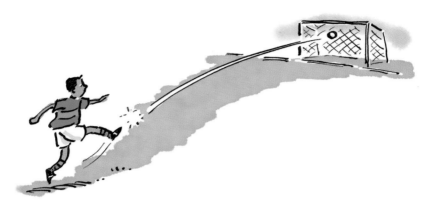

Chapter Four

Training

The team trained every Wednesday after school. They jogged around the field, kicking the ball. They were slowly improving, but they still weren't good enough. Every Saturday, the Caterpillars lost. No one had scored a single goal.

Finally, Ms. Dunleavy decided it was time for a change of tactics. At the next practice, instead of running drills, she turned on her computer.

"Today, we're going to learn about some soccer stars," she told the team. "We'll read about them and watch them playing. I'm sure they can teach you a lot more than I can."

The children had never heard of any of the players. Now, they saw the faces of Mia Hamm, Lionel Messi, Alex Morgan, Marta Vieira da Silva, David Beckham, and many more great players. They learned about their lives and watched them run and score goals. They were amazed by Diego Maradona. And they were on their feet, cheering for Christiano Ronaldo. The great players made it look as if they controlled the ball with a piece of string. They could make it do anything or go anywhere.

23

The children could hardly wait to try some of the skills they had seen. They wanted to run one way while the ball went the other; then, twist sharply back to get the ball again. Most importantly, they wanted to score a goal!

"I'm Maradona!" said Silvio.

The girls joined in, too.

"I'm Mia Hamm!" they cheered

Soccer was fun again.

Chapter Five

Soccer Stars

By the time the last game of the season rolled around, the Caterpillars were better than ever.

"We might even win," said Nuong.

"But if we don't, we'll at least score a goal," said Camilla.

"Maybe two," said Rosa.

Rebecca looked doubtful. "Don't forget, we're playing the Jaguars," she said. "They've won every game so far."

"That's true," said Ms. Dunleavy. "But whatever happens, I'm proud of every one of you. You've all improved so much."

Silvio threw the ball into the air and caught it on his knee. He had seen Maradona do it the same way. For a few seconds, Silvio felt like a soccer star. He even thought he could hear the crowd calling his name—but it was his mom.

"Silvio," she said. "Guess what? I just got a call from the coach of the Jaguars. Their bus has broken down, and they won't be able to make the game. That might not matter to them. They've already won the trophy for best team. But it matters to the Caterpillars because it counts as a win."

"Yay! We won!" shouted everyone. "Finally!"

At the school assembly on Monday, Principal Evans congratulated the Caterpillars and Ms. Dunleavy. "You might not have been the best team," she said, "but you tried hard and you never gave up. The Caterpillars turned into beautiful butterflies!"

Everyone in the school clapped and cheered. The Caterpillars really were soccer stars.

Bill Condon lives New South Wales, Australia. When not writing books, Bill plays tennis, snooker, and Scrabble but hardly ever at the same time. His dream is to receive a wild-card invitation to play tennis at Wimbledon. Bill also wrote *How to Survive in the Jungle, Pipeline News, Race to the Moon,* and *The Human Calculator* for Read! Explore! Imagine! Fiction Readers.

Alasdair Bright lives in Bedford, England. Alasdair's brilliant characters are either created with traditional watercolor and ink or on the computer. Alasdair's work is inspired by Ernest Shepherd, who is best known for his illustration of A.A. Milne's *Winnie-the-Pooh. The Dream Team* is Alasdair's first book for Read! Explore! Imagine! Fiction Readers.